Marx Machiavelli Chesterton Emerson Joyce
Abbott Hardy Montaigne Haggard Cooper Austen
Defoe Melville Hugo
Carroll Christie Eliot Grimm
Stoker Molière
Wilde Maupassant Byron
Engels Schiller
Garnett Einstein Fitzgerald Smith
Goethe Hawthorne Kafka
Cotton Dostoyevsky Hall
Baum Kipling Doyle Willis
Leslie Dumas Henry Nietzsche
Flaubert Turgenev Balzac
Stockton Vatsyayana Crane
Burroughs Whitman Verne
Curtis Tocqueville Gogol Vinci
Homer Widger Tolstoy Busch
Darwin Thoreau
Potter Freud Zola Twain Plato Scott
Lawrence
Kant Jowett Stevenson Dickens Hesse Harte
Andersen Cervantes Burton
London Descartes Voltaire
Poe Aristotle Wells
Hale James Hastings Cooke
Bunner Shakespeare
Richter Chekhov Chambers Irving
Doré Swift Dante da Shaw Wodehouse Benedict Alcott
Pushkin
Newton

tredition®

tredition was established in 2006 by Sandra Latusseck and Soenke Schulz. Based in Hamburg, Germany, tredition offers publishing solutions to authors and publishing houses, combined with worldwide distribution of printed and digital book content. tredition is uniquely positioned to enable authors and publishing houses to create books on their own terms and without conventional manufacturing risks.

For more information please visit: www.tredition.com

TREDITION CLASSICS

This book is part of the TREDITION CLASSICS series. The creators of this series are united by passion for literature and driven by the intention of making all public domain books available in printed format again - worldwide. Most TREDITION CLASSICS titles have been out of print and off the bookstore shelves for decades. At tredition we believe that a great book never goes out of style and that its value is eternal. Several mostly non-profit literature projects provide content to tredition. To support their good work, tredition donates a portion of the proceeds from each sold copy. As a reader of a TREDITION CLASSICS book, you support our mission to save many of the amazing works of world literature from oblivion. See all available books at www.tredition.com.

Project Gutenberg

The content for this book has been graciously provided by Project Gutenberg. Project Gutenberg is a non-profit organization founded by Michael Hart in 1971 at the University of Illinois. The mission of Project Gutenberg is simple: To encourage the creation and distribution of eBooks. Project Gutenberg is the first and largest collection of public domain eBooks.

The Duenna

Richard Brinsley Sheridan

Imprint

This book is part of TREDITION CLASSICS

Author: Richard Brinsley Sheridan
Cover design: Buchgut, Berlin – Germany

Publisher: tredition GmbH, Hamburg - Germany
ISBN: 978-3-8424-6420-9

www.tredition.com
www.tredition.de

The intention of the TREDITION CLASSICS series is to make world literature in the public domain available in printed format. Literary enthusiasts and organizations, such as Project Gutenberg, worldwide have scanned and digitally edited the original texts. tredition has subsequently formatted and redesigned the content into a modern reading layout. Therefore, we cannot guarantee the exact reproduction of the original format of a particular historic edition. Please also note that no modifications have been made to the spelling, therefore it may differ from the orthography used today.

THE DUENNA

A COMIC OPERA

DRAMATIS PERSONAE

AS ORIGINALLY ACTED AT COVENT-GARDEN THEATRE, NOV. 21, 1775

DON FERDINAND *Mr. Mattocks.*
DON JEROME *Mr. Wilson.*
DON ANTONIO *Mr. Dubellamy.*
DON CARLOS *Mr. Leoni.*
ISAAC MENDOZA *Mr. Quick.*
FATHER PAUL *Mr. Mahon.*
FATHER FRANCIS *Mr. Fox.*
FATHER AUGUSTINE *Mr. Baker.*
LOPEZ *Mr. Wewitzer.*
DONNA LOUISA *Mrs. Mattocks.*
DONNA CLARA *Mrs. Cargill.*
THE DUENNA *Mrs. Green.*

Masqueraders, Friars, Porter, Maid, *and* Servants.

SCENE—SEVILLE.

ACT I.

SCENE I.—*The Street before* DON JEROME'S *House.*

Enter LOPEZ, *with a dark lantern.*

Lop. Past three o'clock!—Soh! a notable hour for one of my regular disposition, to be strolling like a bravo through the streets of Seville! Well, of all services, to serve a young lover is the hardest.—Not that I am an enemy to love; but my love and my master's differ strangely.—Don Ferdinand is much too gallant to eat, drink, or sleep:—now my love gives me an appetite—then I am fond of dreaming of my mistress, and I love dearly to toast her.—This cannot be done without good sleep and good liquor: hence my partiality to a feather- bed and a bottle. What a pity, now, that I have not further time, for reflections! but my master expects thee, honest Lopez, to secure his retreat from Donna Clara's window, as I guess.—[*Music without.*] Hey! sure, I heard music! So, so! Who have we here? Oh, Don Antonio, my master's friend, come from the masquerade, to serenade my young mistress, Donna Louisa, I suppose: so! we shall have the old gentleman up presently.—Lest he should miss his son, I had best lose no time in getting to my post. [*Exit.*]

Enter DON ANTONIO, *with* MASQUERADERS *and music.*

SONG.—*Don Ant.*

Tell me, my lute, can thy soft strain
So gently speak thy master's pain?
So softly sing, so humbly sigh,
That, though my sleeping love shall know
Who sings—who sighs below,
Her rosy slumbers shall not fly?
Thus, may some vision whisper more

Than ever I dare speak before.

I. Mas. Antonio, your mistress will never wake, while you sing so dolefully; love, like a cradled infant, is lulled by a sad melody.

Don Ant. I do not wish to disturb her rest.

I. Mas. The reason is, because you know she does not regard you enough to appear, if you awaked her.

Don Ant. Nay, then, I'll convince you. [*Sings.*]

The breath of morn bids hence the night,
Unveil those beauteous eyes, my fair;
For till the dawn of love is there,
I feel no day, I own no light.

DONNA LOUISA—*replies from a window.*

Waking, I heard thy numbers chide,
Waking, the dawn did bless my sight;
'Tis Phoebus sure that woos, I cried,
Who speaks in song, who moves in light.

DON JEROME—*from a window.*

What vagabonds are these I hear,
Fiddling, fluting, rhyming, ranting,
Piping, scraping, whining, canting?
Fly, scurvy minstrels, fly!

TRIO.

Don. Louisa.
Nay, prithee, father, why so rough?

Don Ant.
An humble lover I.

Don Jer.
How durst you, daughter, lend an ear
To such deceitful stuff?
Quick, from the window fly!

Don. Louisa
Adieu, Antonio!

Don Ant
Must you go?

Don. Louisa. & *Don Ant.*
We soon, perhaps, may meet again.
For though hard fortune is our foe,
The God of love will fight for us.

Don Jer.
Reach me the blunderbuss.

Don Ant. & *Don. Louisa.*
The god of love, who knows our pain—

Don Jer.
Hence, or these slugs are through your brain.

[*Exeunt severally.*]

SCENE II—*A Piazza.*

Enter DON FERDINAND *and* LOPEZ.

Lop. Truly, sir, I think that a little sleep once in a week or so——

Don Ferd. Peace, fool! don't mention sleep to me.

Lop. No, no, sir, I don't mention your lowbred, vulgar, sound sleep; but I can't help thinking that a gentle slumber, or half an hour's dozing, if it were only for the novelty of the thing——

Don Ferd. Peace, booby, I say!—Oh, Clara dear, cruel disturber of my rest!

Lop. [*Aside.*] And of mine too.

Don Ferd. 'Sdeath, to trifle with me at such a juncture as this!—now to stand on punctilios!—Love me! I don't believe she ever did.

Lop. [*Aside.*] Nor I either.

Don Ferd. Or is it, that her sex never know their desires for an hour together?

Lop. [*Aside.*] Ah, they know them oftener than they'll own them.

Don Ferd. Is there, in the world, so inconsistent a creature as Clara?

Lop. [*Aside.*] I could name one.

Don Ferd. Yes; the tame fool who submits to her caprice.

Lop. [*Aside.*]I thought he couldn't miss it.

Don Ferd. Is she not capricious, teasing, tyrannical, obstinate, perverse, absurd? ay, a wilderness of faults and follies; her looks are scorn, and her very smiles—'Sdeath! I wish I hadn't mentioned her smiles; for she does smile such beaming loveliness, such fascinating brightness—Oh, death and madness! I shall die if I lose her.

Lop. [*Aside.*] Oh, those damned smiles have undone all!

AIR—*Don Ferd.*

Could I her faults remember,
Forgetting every charm,
Soon would impartial reason
The tyrant love disarm:
But when enraged I number
Each failing of her mind,
Love still suggests each beauty,
And sees—while reason's blind.

Lop. Here comes Don Antonio, sir.

Don Ferd. Well, go you home—I shall be there presently.

Lop. Ah, those cursed smiles! [*Exit*.]

Enter DON ANTONIO.

Don Ferd. Antonio, Lopez tells me he left you chanting before our door—was my father waked?

Don Ant. Yes, yes; he has a singular affection for music; so I left him roaring at his barred window, like the print of Bajazet in the cage. And what brings you out so early?

Don Ferd. I believe I told you, that to-morrow was the day fixed by Don Pedro and Clara's unnatural step-mother, for her to enter a convent, in order that her brat might possess her fortune: made desperate by this, I procured a key to the door, and bribed Clara's maid to leave it unbolted; at two this morning, I entered unperceived, and stole to her chamber—I found her waking and weeping.

Don Ant. Happy Ferdinand!

Don Ferd. 'Sdeath! hear the conclusion.—I was rated as the most confident ruffian, for daring to approach her room at that hour of the night.

Don Ant. Ay, ay, this was at first.

Don Ferd. No such thing! she would not hear a word from me, but threatened to raise her mother, if I did not instantly leave her.

Don Ant. Well, but at last?

Don Ferd. At last! why I was forced to leave the house as I came in.

Don Ant. And did you do nothing to offend her?

Don Ferd. Nothing, as I hope to be saved!—I believe, I might snatch a dozen or two of kisses.

Don Ant. Was that all? well, I think, I never heard of such assurance!

Don Ferd. Zounds! I tell you I behaved with the utmost respect.

Don Ant. O Lord! I don't mean you, but in her. But, hark ye, Ferdinand, did you leave your key with them?

Don Ferd. Yes; the maid who saw me out, took it from the door.

Don Ant. Then, my life for it, her mistress elopes after you.

Don Ferd. Ay, to bless my rival, perhaps. I am in a humour to suspect everybody.—You loved her once, and thought her an angel, as I do now.

Don Ant. Yes, I loved her, till I found she wouldn't love me, and then I discovered that she hadn't a good feature in her face.

AIR.

I ne'er could any lustre see
In eyes that would not look on me;
I ne'er saw nectar on a lip,
But where my own did hope to sip.
Has the maid who seeks my heart
Cheeks of rose, untouch'd by art?
I will own the colour true,
When yielding blushes aid their hue.

Is her hand so soft and pure?
I must press it, to be sure;
Nor can I be certain then,
Till it, grateful, press again.
Must I, with attentive eye,
Watch her heaving bosom sigh?

I will do so, when I see
That heaving bosom sigh for me.

Besides, Ferdinand, you have full security in my love for your sister; help me there, and I can never disturb you with Clara.

Don Ferd. As far as I can, consistently with the honour of our family, you know I will; but there must be no eloping.

Don Ant. And yet, now, you would carry off Clara?

Don Ferd. Ay, that's a different case!—we never mean that others should act to our sisters and wives as we do to others'.—But, tomorrow, Clara is to be forced into a convent.

Don Ant. Well, and am not I so unfortunately circumstanced? To-morrow, your father forces Louisa to marry Isaac, the Portuguese—but come with me, and we'll devise something I warrant.

Don Ferd. I must go home.

Don Ant. Well, adieu!

Don Ferd. But, Don Antonio, if you did not love my sister, you have too much honour and friendship to supplant me with Clara—

AIR—*Don Ant.*

Friendship is the bond of reason;
But if beauty disapprove,
Heaven dissolves all other treason
In the heart that's true to love.

The faith which to my friend I swore,
As a civil oath I view;
But to the charms which I adore,
'Tis religion to be true. [*Exit.*]

Don Ferd. There is always a levity in Antonio's manner of replying to me on this subject that is very alarming.—'Sdeath, if Clara should love him after all.

SONG.

Though cause for suspicion appears,
Yet proofs of her love, too, are strong;
I'm a wretch if I'm right in my fears,
And unworthy of bliss if I'm wrong.
What heart-breaking torments from jealousy flow,
Ah! none but the jealous—the jealous can know!

When blest with the smiles of my fair,
I know not how much I adore:
Those smiles let another but share,
And I wonder I prized them no more!
Then whence can I hope a relief from my woe,
When the falser she seems, still the fonder I grow? [*Exit.*]

SCENE III.—*A Room in* DON JEROME'S *House.*

Enter DONNA LOUISA *and* DUENNA.

Don. Louisa. But, my dear Margaret, my charming Duenna, do you think we shall succeed?

Duen. I tell you again, I have no doubt on't; but it must be instantly put to the trial. Everything is prepared in your room, and for the rest we must trust to fortune.

Don. Louisa. My father's oath was, never to see me till I had consented to— —

Duen. 'Twas thus I overheard him say to his friend, Don Guzman,—*I will demand of her to-morrow, once for all, whether she will consent to marry Isaac Mendoza; if she hesitates, I will make a solemn oath never to see or speak to her till she returns to her duty.*—These were his words.

Don. Louisa. And on his known obstinate adherence to what he has once said, you have formed this plan for my escape.—But have you secured my maid in our interest?

Duen. She is a party in the whole; but remember, if we succeed, you resign all right and title in little Isaac, the Jew, over to me.

Don. Louisa. That I do with all my soul; get him if you can, and I shall wish you joy most heartily. He is twenty times as rich as my poor Antonio.

AIR.

Thou canst not boast of fortune's store,
My love, while me they wealthy call:
But I was glad to find thee poor—
For with my heart I'd give thee all.
And then the grateful youth shall own

I loved him for himself alone.

But when his worth my hand shall gain,
No word or look of mine shall show
That I the smallest thought retain
Of what my bounty did bestow;
Yet still his grateful heart shall own
I loved him for himself alone.

Duen. I hear Don Jerome coming.—Quick, give me the last letter I brought you from Antonio—you know that is to be the ground of my dismission.—I must slip out to seal it up, as undelivered. [*Exit*.]

Enter DON JEROME *and* DON FERDINAND.

Don Jer. What, I suppose you have been serenading too! Eh, disturbing some peaceable neighbourhood with villainous catgut and lascivious piping! Out on't! you set your sister, here, a vile example; but I come to tell you, madam, that I'll suffer no more of these midnight incantations—these amorous orgies, that steal the senses in the hearing; as, they say, Egyptian embalmers serve mummies, extracting the brain through the ears. However, there's an end of your frolics.—Isaac Mendoza will be here presently, and to-morrow you shall marry him.

Don. Louisa. Never, while I have life!

Don Ferd. Indeed, sir, I wonder how you can think of such a man for a son-in-law.

Don Jer. Sir, you are very kind to favour me with your sentiments— and pray, what is your objection to him?

Don Ferd. He is a Portuguese, in the first place.

Don Jer. No such thing, boy; he has forsworn his country.

Don. Louisa. He is a Jew.

Don Jer. Another mistake: he has been a Christian these six weeks.

Don Ferd. Ay, he left his old religion for an estate, and has not had time to get a new one.

Don. Louisa. But stands like a dead wall between church and synagogue, or like the blank leaves between the Old and New Testament.

Don Jer. Anything more?

Don Ferd. But the most remarkable part of his character is his passion for deceit and tricks of cunning.

Don. Louisa. Though at the same time the fool predominates so much over the knave, that I am told he is generally the dupe of his own art.

Don Ferd. True; like an unskilful gunner, he usually misses his aim, and is hurt by the recoil of his own piece.

Don Jer. Anything more?

Don. Louisa. To sum up all, he has the worst fault a husband can have—he's not my choice.

Don Jer. But you are his; and choice on one side is sufficient—two lovers should never meet in marriage—be you sour as you please, he is sweet-tempered; and for your good fruit, there's nothing like ingrafting on a crab.

Don. Louisa. I detest him as a lover, and shall ten times more as a husband.

Don Jer. I don't know that-marriage generally makes a great change— but, to cut the matter short, will you have him or not?

Don. Louisa. There is nothing else I could disobey you in.

Don Jer. Do you value your father's peace?

Don. Louisa. So much, that I will not fasten on him the regret of making an only daughter wretched.

Don Jer. Very well, ma'am, then mark me—never more will I see or converse with you till you return to your duty—no reply—this and your chamber shall be your apartments; I never will stir out without leaving you under lock and key, and when I'm at home no creature can approach you but through my library: we'll try who can be most obstinate. Out of my sight!—there remain till you know your duty. [*Pushes her out.*]

Don Ferd_. Surely, sir, my sister's inclinations should be consulted in a matter of this kind, and some regard paid to Don Antonio, being my particular friend.

Don Jer. That, doubtless, is a very great recommendation!—I certainly have not paid sufficient respect to it.

Don Ferd. There is not a man living I would sooner choose for a brother-in-law.

Don Jer. Very possible; and if you happen to have e'er a sister, who is not at the same time a daughter of mine, I'm sure I shall have no objection to the relationship; but at present, if you please, we'll drop the subject.

Don Ferd. Nay, sir, 'tis only my regard for my sister makes me speak.

Don Jer. Then, pray sir, in future, let your regard for your father make you hold your tongue.

Don Ferd. I have done, sir. I shall only add a wish that you would reflect what at our age you would have felt, had you been crossed in your affection for the mother of her you are so severe to.

Don Jer. Why, I must confess I had a great affection for your mother's ducats, but that was all, boy. I married her for her fortune, and she took me in obedience to her father, and a very happy couple we were. We never expected any love from one another, and so we were never disappointed. If we grumbled a little now and then, it was soon over, for we were never fond enough to quarrel; and when the good woman died, why, why,—I had as lieve she had lived, and I wish every widower in Seville could say the same. I shall now go and get the key of this dressing-room—so, good son, if you have any lecture in support of disobedience to give your sister, it must be brief; so make the best of your time, d'ye hear? [*Exit.*]

Don Ferd. I fear, indeed, my friend Antonio has little to hope for; however, Louisa has firmness, and my father's anger will probably only increase her affection.—In our intercourse with the world, it is natural for us to dislike those who are innocently the cause of our distress; but in the heart's attachment a woman never likes a man with ardour till she has suffered for his sake.—[*Noise.*] So! what bustle is here—between my father and the Duenna too, I'll e'en get out of the way. [*Exit.*]

Re-enter DON JEROME *with a letter, pulling in* DUENNA.

Don Jer. I'm astonished! I'm thunderstruck! here's treachery with a vengeance! You, Antonio's creature, and chief manager of this plot for my daughter's eloping!—you, that I placed here as a scarecrow?

Duen. What?

Don Jer. A scarecrow—to prove a decoy-duck! What have you to say for yourself?

Duen. Well, sir, since you have forced that letter from me, and discovered my real sentiments, I scorn to renounce them.—I am Antonio's friend, and it was my intention that your daughter should have served you as all such old tyrannical sots should be served—I delight in the tender passions and would befriend all under their influence.

Don Jer. The tender passions! yes, they would become those impenetrable features! Why, thou deceitful hag! I placed thee as a guard to the rich blossoms of my daughter's beauty. I thought that dragon's front of thine would cry aloof to the sons of gallantry: steel traps and spring guns seemed writ in every wrinkle of it.—But you shall quit my house this instant. The tender passions, indeed! go, thou wanton sibyl, thou amorous woman of Endor, go!

Duen. You base, scurrilous, old—but I won't demean myself by naming what you are.—Yes, savage, I'll leave your den; but I suppose you don't mean to detain my apparel—I may have my things, I presume?

Don Jer. I took you, mistress, with your wardrobe on—what have you pilfered, eh?

Duen. Sir, I must take leave of my mistress; she has valuables of mine: besides, my cardinal and veil are in her room.

Don Jer. Your veil, forsooth! what, do you dread being gazed at? or are you afraid of your complexion? Well, go take your leave, and get your veil and cardinal! so! you quit the house within these five minutes.—In—in—quick!—[*Exit* DUENNA.] Here was a precious plot of mischief!—these are the comforts daughters bring us!

AIR.

If a daughter you have, she's the plague of your life,
No peace shall you know, though you've buried your wife!
At twenty she mocks at the duty you taught her—
Oh, what a plague is an obstinate daughter!
Sighing and whining,
Dying and pining,
Oh, what a plague is an obstinate daughter!

When scarce in their teens they have wit to perplex us,
With letters and lovers for ever they vex us;
While each still rejects the fair suitor you've brought her;
Oh, what a plague is an obstinate daughter!
Wrangling and jangling, Flouting and pouting,
Oh, what a plague is an obstinate daughter!

Re-enter DONNA LOUISA, *dressed as* DUENNA, *with cardinal and veil, seeming to cry*.

This way, mistress, this way.—What, I warrant a tender parting; so! tears of turpentine down those deal cheeks.—Ay, you may well hide your head—yes, whine till your heart breaks! but I'll not hear one word of excuse—so you are right to be dumb. This way, this way. [*Exeunt*.]

Re-enter DUENNA.

Duen. So, speed you well, sagacious Don Jerome! Oh rare effects of passion and obstinacy! Now shall I try whether I can't play the fine lady as well as my mistress, and if I succeed, I may be a fine lady for the rest of my life—I'll lose no time to equip myself. [*Exit*.]

SCENE IV.—*The Court before* DON JEROME'S _House.

Enter_ DON JEROME *and* DONNA LOUISA.

Don Jer. Come, mistress, there is your way—the world lies before you, so troop, thou antiquated Eve, thou original sin! Hold, yonder is some fellow skulking; perhaps it is Antonio—go to him, d'ye hear, and tell him to make you amends, and as he has got you turned away, tell him I say it is but just he should take you himself; go—[*Exit* DONNA LOUISA.] So! I am rid of her, thank heaven! and now I shall be able to keep my oath, and confine my daughter with better security. [*Exit*].

SCENE V.-_The Piazza.

Enter_ DONNA CLARA *and* MAID.

Maid. But where, madam, is it you intend to go?

Don. Clara. Anywhere to avoid the selfish violence of my mother-in- law, and Ferdinand's insolent importunity.

Maid. Indeed, ma'am, since we have profited by Don Ferdinand's key, in making our escape, I think we had best find him, if it were only to thank him.

Don. Clara. No—he has offended me exceedingly. [*Retires*].

Enter DONNA LOUISA.

Don. Louisa. So I have succeeded in being turned out of doors—but how shall I find Antonio? I dare not inquire for him, for fear of being discovered; I would send to my friend Clara, but then I doubt her prudery would condemn me.

Maid. Then suppose, ma'am, you were to try if your friend Donna Louisa would not receive you?

Don. Clara. No, her notions of filial duty are so severe, she would certainly betray me.

Don. Louisa. Clara is of a cold temper, and would think this step of mine highly forward.

Don. Clara. Louisa's respect for her father is so great, she would not credit the unkindness of mine.

[DONNA LOUISA *turns and sees* DONNA CLARA *and* MAID.]

Don. Louisa. Ha! who are those? sure one is Clara—if it be, I'll trust her. Clara! [*Advances.*]

Don. Clara. Louisa! and in masquerade too!

Don. Louisa. You will be more surprised when I tell you, that I have run away from my father.

Don. Clara. Surprised indeed! and I should certainly chide you most horridly, only that I have just run away from mine.

Don. Louisa. My dear Clara! [*Embrace.*]

Don. Clara. Dear sister truant! and whither are you going?

Don. Louisa. To find the man I love, to be sure; and, I presume, you would have no aversion to meet with my brother?

Don. Clara. Indeed I should: he has behaved so ill to me, I don't believe I shall ever forgive him.

AIR.

When sable night, each drooping plant restoring,
Wept o'er the flowers her breath did cheer,
As some sad widow o'er her babe deploring,
Wakes its beauty with a tear;
When all did sleep whose weary hearts did borrow
One hour from love and care to rest,
Lo! as I press'd my couch in silent sorrow,
My lover caught me to his breast!
He vow'd he came to save me
From those who would enslave me!
Then kneeling, Kisses stealing,
Endless faith he swore;
But soon I chid him thence,
For had his fond pretence
Obtain'd one favour then,
And he had press'd again,
I fear'd my treacherous heart might grant him more.

Don. Louisa. Well, for all this, I would have sent him to plead his pardon, but that I would not yet awhile have him know of my flight. And where do you hope to find protection?

Don. Clara. The Lady Abbess of the convent of St. Catherine is a relation and kind friend of mine—I shall be secure with her, and you had best go thither with me.

Don. Louisa. No; I am determined to find Antonio first; and, as I live, here comes the very man I will employ to seek him for me.

Don. Clara. Who is he? he's a strange figure.

Don. Louisa. Yes; that sweet creature is the man whom my father has fixed on for my husband.

Don. Clara. And will you speak to him? are you mad?

Don. Louisa. He is the fittest man in the world for my purpose; for, though I was to have married him to-morrow, he is the only man in Seville who, I am sure, never saw me in his life.

Don. Clara. And how do you know him?

Don. Louisa. He arrived but yesterday, and he was shown to me from the window, as he visited my father.

Don. Clara. Well, I'll begone.

Don. Louisa. Hold, my dear Clara—a thought has struck me: will you give me leave to borrow your name, as I see occasion?

Don. Clara. It will but disgrace you; but use it as you please: I dare not stay.—[*Going.*]—But, Louisa, if you should see your brother, be sure you don't inform him that I have taken refuge with the Dame Prior of the convent of St. Catherine, on the left hand side of the piazza which leads to the church of St. Anthony.

Don. Louisa. Ha! ha! ha! I'll be very particular in my directions where he may not find you.—[*Exeunt* DONNA CLARA *and* MAID.]—So! My swain, yonder, has, done admiring himself, and draws nearer. [*Retires.*]

Enter ISAAC *and* DON CARLOS.

Isaac. [*Looking in a pocket-glass.*] I tell you, friend Carlos, I will please myself in the habit of my chin.

Don Car. But, my dear friend, how can you think to please a lady with such a face?

Isaac. Why, what's the matter with the face? I think it is a very engaging face; and, I am sure, a lady must have very little taste who could dislike my beard.—[*Sees* DONNA LOUISA.]—See now! I'll die if here is not a little damsel struck with it already.

Don. Louisa. Signor, are you disposed to oblige a lady who greatly wants your assistance? [*Unveils.*]

Isaac. Egad, a very pretty black-eyed girl! she has certainly taken a fancy to me, Carlos. First, ma'am, I must beg the favour of your name.

Don. Louisa. [*Aside.*] So! it's well I am provided.—[*Aloud.*]—My name, sir, is Donna Clara d'Almanza.

Isaac. What? Don Guzman's daughter? I'faith, I just now heard she was missing.

Don. Louisa. But sure, sir, you have too much gallantry and honour to betray me, whose fault is love?

Isaac. So! a passion for me! poor girl! Why, ma'am, as for betraying you, I don't see how I could get anything by it; so, you may rely on my honour; but as for your love, I am sorry your case is so desperate.

Don. Louisa. Why so, signor?

Isaac. Because I am positively engaged to another—an't I, Carlos?

Don. Louisa. Nay, but hear me.

Isaac. No, no; what should I hear for? It is impossible for me to court you in an honourable way; and for anything else, if I were to comply now, I suppose you have some ungrateful brother, or cousin, who would want to cut my throat for my civility—so, truly, you had best go home again.

Don. Louisa. [*Aside.*] Odious wretch!—[*Aloud.*]—But, good signor, it is Antonio d'Ercilla, on whose account I have eloped.

Isaac. How! what! it is not with me, then, that you are in love?

Don. Louisa. No, indeed, it is not.

Isaac. Then you are a forward, impertinent simpleton! and I shall certainly acquaint your father.

Don. Louisa. Is this your gallantry?

Isaac. Yet hold—Antonio d'Ercilla, did you say? egad, I may make something of this—Antonio d'Ercilla?

Don. Louisa. Yes; and if ever you wish to prosper in love, you will bring me to him.

Isaac. By St. Iago and I will too!—Carlos, this Antonio is one who rivals me (as I have heard) with Louisa—now, if I could hamper him with this girl, I should have the field to myself; hey, Carlos! A lucky thought, isn't it?

Don Car. Yes, very good—very good!

Isaac. Ah! this little brain is never at a loss—cunning Isaac! cunning rogue! Donna Clara, will you trust yourself awhile to my friend's direction?

Don. Louisa. May I rely on you, good signor?

Don. Car. Lady, it is impossible I should deceive you.

AIR.

Had I a heart for falsehood framed,
I ne'er could injure you;
For though your tongue no promise claim'd,
Your charms would make me true.
To you no soul shall bear deceit,
No stranger offer wrong;
But friends in all the aged you'll meet,
And lovers in the young.

But when they learn that you have blest
Another with your heart,
They'll bid aspiring passion rest,
And act a brother's part:
Then, lady, dread not here deceit,
Nor fear to suffer wrong;

For friends in all the aged you'll meet,
And brothers in the young.

Isaac. Conduct the lady to my lodgings, Carlos; I must haste to Don Jerome. Perhaps you know Louisa, ma'am. She's divinely handsome, isn't she?

Don. Louisa. You must excuse me not joining with you.

Isaac. Why I have heard it on all hands.

Don. Louisa. Her father is uncommonly partial to her; but I believe you will find she has rather a matronly air.

Isaac. Carlos, this is all envy.—You pretty girls never speak well of one another.—[*To* DON CARLOS.] Hark ye, find out Antonio, and I'll saddle him with this scrape, I warrant. Oh, 'twas the luckiest thought! Donna Clara, your very obedient. Carlos, to your post.

DUET.

Isaac.
My mistress expects me, and I must go to her,
Or how can I hope for a smile?

Don. Louisa.
Soon may you return a prosperous wooer,
But think what I suffer the while.
Alone, and away from the man whom I love,
In strangers I'm forced to confide.

Isaac.
Dear lady, my friend you may trust, and he'll prove
Your servant, protector, and guide.

AIR.

Don Car.
Gentle maid, ah! why suspect me?
Let me serve thee—then reject me.

Canst thou trust, and I deceive thee?
Art thou sad, and shall I grieve thee?
Gentle maid, ah I why suspect me?
Let me serve thee—then reject me.

TRIO.

Don. Louisa.
Never mayst thou happy be,
If in aught thou'rt false to me.

Isaac.
Never may he happy be,
If in aught he's false to thee.

Don Car.
Never may I happy be,
If in aught I'm false to thee.

Don. Louisa.
Never mayst thou, &c.

Isaac.
Never may he, &c.

Don Car.
Never may I, &c. [*Exeunt.*]

ACT II.

SCENE I.—*A Library in* **DON JEROME'S** *House.*

Enter DON JEROME *and* ISAAC.

Don Jer. Ha! ha! ha! run away from her father! has she given him the slip? Ha! ha! ha! poor Don Guzman!

Isaac. Ay; and I am to conduct her to Antonio; by which means you see I shall hamper him so that he can give me no disturbance with your daughter—this is a trap, isn't it? a nice stroke of cunning, hey?

Don Jer. Excellent! excellent I yes, yes, carry her to him, hamper him by all means, ha! ha! ha! Poor Don Guzman! an old fool! imposed on by a girl!

Isaac. Nay, they have the cunning of serpents, that's the truth on't.

Don Jer. Psha! they are cunning only when they have fools to deal with. Why don't my girl play me such a trick? Let her cunning overreach my caution, I say—hey, little Isaac!

Isaac. True, true; or let me see any of the sex make a fool of me!—No, no, egad! little Solomon (as my aunt used to call me) understands tricking a little too well.

Don Jer. Ay, but such a driveller as Don Guzman!

Isaac. And such a dupe as Antonio!

Don Jer. True; never were seen such a couple of credulous simpletons! But come, 'tis time you should see my daughter—you must carry on the siege by yourself, friend Isaac.

Isaac. Sir, you'll introduce— —

Don Jer. No—I have sworn a solemn oath not to see or to speak to her till she renounces her disobedience; win her to that, and she gains a father and a husband at once.

Isaac. Gad, I shall never be able to deal with her alone; nothing keeps me in such awe as perfect beauty—now there is something consoling and encouraging in ugliness.

SONG

Give Isaac the nymph who no beauty can boast,
But health and good humour to make her his toast;
If straight, I don't mind whether slender or fat,
And six feet or four—we'll ne'er quarrel for that.

Whate'er her complexion, I vow I don't care;
If brown, it is lasting—more pleasing, if fair:
And though in her face I no dimples should see,
Let her smile—and each dell is a dimple to me.

Let her locks be the reddest that ever were seen,
And her eyes may be e'en any colour but green;
For in eyes, though so various in lustre and hue,
I swear I've no choice—only let her have two.

'Tis true I'd dispense with a throne on her back,
And white teeth, I own, are genteeler than black;
A little round chin too's a beauty, I've heard;
But I only desire she mayn't have a beard.

Don Jer. You will change your note, my friend, when you've seen Louisa.

Isaac. Oh, Don Jerome, the honour of your alliance— —

Don Jer. Ay, but her beauty will affect you—she is, though I say it who am her father, a very prodigy. There you will see features with an eye like mine—yes, i'faith, there is a kind of wicked sparkling—sometimes of a roguish brightness, that shows her to be my own.

Isaac. Pretty rogue!

Don Jer. Then, when she smiles, you'll see a little dimple in one cheek only; a beauty it is certainly, yet, you shall not say which is prettiest, the cheek with the dimple, or the cheek without.

Isaac. Pretty rogue!

Don Jer. Then the roses on those cheeks are shaded with a sort of velvet down, that gives a delicacy to the glow of health.

Isaac. Pretty rogue!

Don Jer. Her skin pure dimity, yet more fair, being spangled here and there with a golden freckle.

Isaac. Charming pretty rogue! pray how is the tone of her voice?

Don Jer. Remarkably pleasing—but if you could prevail on her to sing, you would be enchanted—she is a nightingale—a Virginia nightingale! But come, come; her maid shall conduct you to her antechamber.

Isaac. Well, egad, I'll pluck up resolution, and meet her frowns intrepidly.

Don Jer. Ay! woo her briskly—win her, and give me a proof of your address, my little Solomon.

Isaac. But hold—I expect my friend Carlos to call on me here. If he comes, will you send him to me?

Don Jer. I will. Lauretta!—[*Calls*.]—Come—she'll show you to the room. What! do you droop? here's a mournful face to make love with! [*Exeunt*.]

SCENE II.—DONNA LOUISA'S *Dressing-Room.*

Enter ISAAC *and* MAID.

Maid. Sir, my mistress will wait on you presently.

[*Goes to the door.*]

Isaac. When she's at leisure—don't hurry her.—[*Exit* MAID.]—I wish I had ever practised a love-scene—I doubt I shall make a poor figure—I couldn't be more afraid if I was going before the Inquisition. So, the door opens—yes, she's coming—the very rustling of her silk has a disdainful sound.

Enter DUENNA *dressed* as DONNA LOUISA.

Now dar'n't I look round, for the soul of me—her beauty will certainly strike me dumb if I do. I wish she'd speak first.

Duen. Sir, I attend your pleasure.

Isaac. [*Aside.*] So! the ice is broke, and a pretty civil beginning too!—[*Aloud.*] Hem! madam—miss—I'm all attention.

Duen. Nay, sir, 'tis I who should listen, and you propose.

Isaac. [*Aside.*] Egad, this isn't so disdainful neither—I believe I may venture to look. No—I dar'n't—one glance of those roguish sparklers would fix me again.

Duen. You seem thoughtful, sir. Let me persuade you to sit down.

Isaac. [*Aside.*] So, so; she mollifies apace—she's struck with my figure! this attitude has had its effect.

Duen. Come, sir, here's a chair.

Isaac. Madam, the greatness of your goodness overpowers me—that a lady so lovely should deign to turn her beauteous eyes on me so.

[*She takes his hand, he turns and sees her.*]

Duen. You seem surprised at my condescension.

Isaac. Why, yes, madam, I am a little surprised at it.—[*Aside.*] Zounds! this can never be Louisa—she's as old as my mother!

Duen. But former prepossessions give way to my father's commands.

Isaac. [*Aside.*] Her father! Yes, 'tis she then.—Lord, Lord; how blind some parents are!

Duen. Signor Isaac!

Isaac. [*Aside.*] Truly, the little damsel was right—she has rather a matronly air, indeed! ah! 'tis well my affections are fixed on her fortune, and not her person.

Duen. Signor, won't you sit? [*She sits.*]

Isaac. Pardon me, madam, I have scarce recovered my astonishment at your condescension, madam.—[*Aside.*] She has the devil's own dimples, to be sure!

Duen. I do not wonder, sir, that you are surprised at my affability— I own, signor, that I was vastly prepossessed against you, and, being teased by my father, I did give some encouragement to Antonio; but then, sir, you were described to me as quite a different person.

Isaac. Ay, and so you were to me, upon my soul, madam.

Duen. But when I saw you I was never more struck in my life.

Isaac. That was just my case, too, madam: I was struck all of a heap, for my part.

Duen. Well, sir, I see our misapprehension has been mutual—you expected to find me haughty and averse, and I was taught to believe you a little black, snub-nosed fellow, without person, manners, or address.

Isaac. [*Aside.*] Egad, I wish she had answered her picture as well!

Duen. But, sir, your air is noble—something so liberal in your carriage, with so penetrating an eye, and so bewitching a smile!

Isaac. [*Aside.*] Egad, now I look at her again, I don't think she is so ugly!

Duen. So little like a Jew, and so much like a gentleman!

Isaac. [*Aside.*] Well, certainly, there is something pleasing in the tone of her voice.

Duen. You will pardon this breach of decorum in praising you thus, but my joy at being so agreeably deceived has given me such a flow of spirits!

Isaac. Oh, dear lady, may I thank those dear lips for this goodness?—[*Kisses her.*] [*Aside.*]Why she has a pretty sort of velvet down, that's the truth on't.

Duen. O sir, you have the most insinuating manner, but indeed you should get rid of that odious beard—one might as well kiss a hedgehog.

Isaac. [*Aside.*] Yes, ma'am, the razor wouldn't be amiss—for either of us.—[*Aloud.*] Could you favour me with a song?

Duen. Willingly, though I'm rather hoarse—ahem![*Begins to sing.*]

Isaac. [*Aside.*] Very like a Virginia nightingale!—[*Aloud.*] Ma'am, I perceive you're hoarse—I beg you will not distress— —

Duen. Oh, not in the least distressed. Now, sir.

SONG.

When a tender maid
Is first assay'd
By some admiring swain.
How her blushes rise
If she meet his eyes,
While he unfolds his pain!
If he takes her hand, she trembles quite!
Touch her lips, and she swoons outright!
While a pit-a-pat, &c.
Her heart avows her fright.

But in time appear
Fewer signs of fear;
The youth she boldly views:
If her hand he grasp,
Or her bosom clasp,
No mantling blush ensues!
Then to church well pleased the lovers move,
While her smiles her contentment prove;
And a pit-a-pat, &c. Her heart avows her love.

Isaac. Charming, ma'am! enchanting! and, truly, your notes put me in mind of one that's very dear to me—a lady, indeed, whom you greatly resemble!

Duen. How I is there, then, another so dear to you?

Isaac. Oh, no, ma'am, you mistake; it was my mother I meant.

Duen. Come, sir, I see you are amazed and confounded at my condescension, and know not what to say.

Isaac. It is very true, indeed, ma'am; but it is a judgment, I look on it as a judgment on me, for delaying to urge the time when you'll permit me to complete my happiness, by acquainting Don Jerome with your condescension.

Duen. Sir, I must frankly own to you, that I can never be yours with my father's consent.

Isaac. Good lack! how so?

Duen. When my father, in his passion, swore he would never see me again till I acquiesced in his will, I also made a vow, that I would never take a husband from his hand; nothing shall make me break that oath: but if you have spirit and contrivance enough to carry me off without his knowledge, I'm yours.

Isaac. Hum!

Duen. Nay, sir, if you hesitate——

Isaac. [*Aside.*] I'faith no bad whim this!—If I take her at her word, I shall secure her fortune, and avoid making any settlement in return; thus I shall not only cheat the lover, but the father too. Oh, cunning rogue, Isaac! ay, ay, let this little brain alone! Egad, I'll take her in the mind!

Duen. Well, sir, what's your determination?

Isaac. Madam, I was dumb only from rapture—I applaud your spirit, and joyfully close with your proposal; for which thus let me, on this lily hand, express my gratitude.

Duen. Well, sir, you must get my father's consent to walk with me in the garden. But by no means inform him of my kindness to you.

Isaac. No, to be sure, that would spoil all: but, trust me when tricking is the word—let me alone for a piece of cunning; this very day you shall be out of his power.

Duen. Well, I leave the management of it all to you; I perceive plainly, sir, that you are not one that can be easily outwitted.

Isaac. Egad, you're right, madam—you're right, i'faith.

Re-enter MAID.

Maid. Here's a gentleman at the door, who begs permission to speak with Signor Isaac.

Isaac. A friend of mine, ma'am, and a trusty friend—let him come in—[*Exit* MAID.] He's one to be depended on, ma'am.

Enter DON CARLOS.

So coz. [*Talks apart with* DON CARLOS.]

Don Car. I have left Donna Clara at your lodgings, but can nowhere find Antonio.

Isaac. Well, I will search him out myself. Carlos, you rogue, I thrive, I prosper!

Don Car. Where is your mistress?

Isaac. There, you booby, there she stands.

Don Car. Why, she's damned ugly!

Isaac. Hush! [*Stops his mouth*.]

Duen. What is your friend saying, signor?

Isaac. Oh, ma'am, he is expressing his raptures at such charms as he never saw before. Eh, Carlos?

Don Car. Ay,—such as I never saw before, indeed!

Duen. You are a very obliging gentleman. Well, Signor Isaac, I believe we had better part for the present. Remember our plan.

Isaac. Oh, ma'am, it is written in my heart, fixed as the image of those divine beauties. Adieu, idol of my soul!—yet once more permit me— —[*Kisses her.*]

Duen. Sweet, courteous sir, adieu!

Isaac. Your slave eternally! Come, Carlos, say something civil at taking leave.

Don Car. I'faith, Isaac, she is the hardest woman to compliment I ever saw; however, I'll try something I had studied for the occasion.

SONG.

Ah! sure a pair was never seen
So justly form'd to meet by nature!
The youth excelling so in mien,
The maid in ev'ry grace of feature.
Oh, how happy are such lovers,
When kindred beauties each discovers;
For surely she Was made for thee,
And thou to bless this lovely creature!

So mild your looks, your children thence
Will early learn the task of duty—
The boys with all their father's sense,
The girls with all their mother's beauty!
Oh, how happy to inherit
At once such graces and such spirit!
Thus while you live
May fortune give
Each blessing equal to your merit! [*Exeunt.*]

SCENE III.—*A Library in* DON JEROME'S *House.*

DON JEROME *and* DON FERDINAND *discovered.*

Don Jer. Object to Antonio! I have said it. His poverty, can you acquit him of that?

Don Ferd. Sir, I own he is not over rich; but he is of as ancient and honourable a family as any in the kingdom.

Don Jer. Yes, I know the beggars are a very ancient family in most kingdoms; but never in great repute, boy.

Don Ferd. Antonio, sir, has many amiable qualities.

Don Jer. But he is poor; can you clear him of that, I say? Is he not a gay, dissipated rake, who has squandered his patrimony?

Don Ferd. Sir, he inherited but little; and that his generosity, more than his profuseness, has stripped him of; but he has never sullied his honour, which, with his title, has outlived his means.

Don Jer. Psha! you talk like a blockhead! nobility, without an estate, is as ridiculous as gold lace on a frieze coat.

Don Ferd. This language, sir, would better become a Dutch or English trader than a Spaniard.

Don Jer. Yes; and those Dutch and English traders, as you call them, are the wiser people. Why, booby, in England they were formerly as nice, as to birth and family, as we are: but they have long discovered what a wonderful purifier gold is; and now, no one there regards pedigree in anything but a horse. Oh, here comes Isaac! I hope he has prospered in his suit.

Don Ferd. Doubtless, that agreeable figure of his must have helped his suit surprisingly.

Don Jer. How now? [DON FERDINAND *walks aside.*]

Enter ISAAC.

Well, my friend, have you softened her?

Isaac. Oh, yes; I have softened her.

Don Jer. What, does she come to?

Isaac. Why, truly, she was kinder than I expected to find her.

Don Jer. And the dear little angel was civil, eh?

Isaac. Yes, the pretty little angel was very civil.

Don Jer. I'm transported to hear it! Well, and you were astonished at her beauty, hey?

Isaac. I was astonished, indeed! Pray, how old is Miss?

Don Jer. How old? let me see—eight and twelve—she is twenty.

Isaac. Twenty?

Don Jer. Ay, to a month.

Isaac. Then, upon my soul, she is the oldest-looking girl of her age in Christendom!

Don Jer. Do you think so? But, I believe, you will not see a prettier girl.

Isaac. Here and there one.

Don Jer. Louisa has the family face.

Isaac. [*Aside*.] Yes, egad, I should have taken it for a family face, and one that has been in the family some time, too.

Don Jer. She has her father's eyes.

Isaac. [*Aside*.]Truly, I should have guessed them to have been so! If she had her mother's spectacles, I believe she would not see the worse.

Don Jer. Her aunt Ursula's nose, and her grandmother's forehead, to a hair.

Isaac. [*Aside*.]Ay, 'faith, and her grandfather's chin, to a hair.

Don Jer. Well, if she was but as dutiful as she's handsome—and hark ye, friend Isaac, she is none of your made-up beauties—her charms are of the lasting kind.

Isaac. I'faith, so they should—for if she be but twenty now, she may double her age before her years will overtake her face.

Don Jer. Why, zounds, Master Isaac! you are not sneering, are you?

Isaac. Why now, seriously, Don Jerome, do you think your daughter handsome?

Don Jer. By this light, she's as handsome a girl as any in Seville.

Isaac. Then, by these eyes, I think her as plain a woman as ever I beheld.

Don Jer. By St. Iago! you must be blind.

Isaac. No, no; 'tis you are partial.

Don Jer. How! have I neither sense nor taste? If a fair skin, fine eyes, teeth of ivory, with a lovely bloom, and a delicate shape,—if these, with a heavenly voice and a world of grace, are not charms, I know not what you call beautiful.

Isaac. Good lack, with what eyes a father sees! As I have life, she is the very reverse of all this: as for the dimity skin you told me of, I swear 'tis a thorough nankeen as ever I saw! for her eyes, their utmost merit is not squinting—for her teeth, where there is one of ivory, its neighbour is pure ebony, black and white alternately, just like the keys of a harpsichord. Then, as to her singing, and heavenly voice—by this hand, she has a shrill, cracked pipe, that sounds for all the world like a child's trumpet.

Don Jer. Why, you little Hebrew scoundrel, do you mean to insult me? Out of my house, I say!

Don Ferd. [*Coming forward.*] Dear sir, what's the matter?

Don Jer. Why, this Israelite here has the impudence to say your sister's ugly.

Don Ferd. He must be either blind or insolent.

Isaac. [*Aside.*]So, I find they are all in a story. Egad, I believe I have gone too far!

Don Ferd. Sure, sir, there must be some mistake; it can't be my sister whom he has seen.

Don Jer. 'Sdeath! you are as great a fool as he! What mistake can there be? Did not I lock up Louisa, and haven't I the key in my own pocket? and didn't her maid show him into the dressing-room? and yet you talk of a mistake! No, the Portuguese meant to insult me—and, but that this roof protects him, old as I am, this sword should do me justice.

Isaac. I[*Aside.*] must get off as well as I can—her fortune is not the less handsome.

DUET.

Isaac.
Believe me, good sir, I ne'er meant to offend;
My mistress I love, and I value my friend
To win her and wed her is still my request,
For better for worse—and I swear I don't jest.

Don Jer.
Zounds! you'd best not provoke me, my rage is so high!

Isaac.
Hold him fast, I beseech you, his rage is so high!
Good sir, you're too hot, and this place I must fly.

Don Jer.
You're a knave and a sot, and this place you'd best fly.

Isaac. Don Jerome, come now, let us lay aside all joking, and be serious.

Don Jer. How?

Isaac. Ha! ha! ha! I'll be hanged if you haven't taken my abuse of your daughter seriously.

Don Jer. You meant it so, did not you?

Isaac. O mercy, no! a joke—just to try how angry it would make you.

Don Jer. Was that all, i'faith? I didn't know you had been such a wag. Ha! ha! ha! By St. Iago! you made me very angry, though. Well, and you do think Louisa handsome?

Isaac. Handsome! Venus de Medicis was a sybil to her.

Don Jer. Give me your hand, you little jocose rogue! Egad, I thought we had been all off.

Don Ferd. [*Aside*.] So! I was in hopes this would have been a quarrel; but I find the Jew is too cunning.

Don Jer. Ay, this gust of passion has made me dry—I am seldom ruffled. Order some wine in the next room—let us drink the poor girl's health. Poor Louisa! ugly, eh! ha! ha! ha! 'twas a very good joke, indeed!

Isaac. [*Aside*.] And a very true one, for all that.

Don Jer, And, Ferdinand, I insist upon your drinking success to my friend.

Don Ferd. Sir, I will drink success to my friend with all my heart.

Don Jer. Come, little Solomon, if any sparks of anger had remained, this would be the only way to quench them.

TRIO.

A bumper of good liquor
Will end a contest quicker
Than justice, judge, or vicar;
So fill a cheerful glass,
And let good humour pass.
But if more deep the quarrel,
Why, sooner drain the barrel
Than be the hateful fellow
That's crabbed when he's mellow.

A bumper, &c. [*Exeunt.*]

SCENE IV.—ISAAC'S *Lodgings.*

Enter DONNA LOUISA.

Don. Louisa. Was ever truant daughter so whimsically circumstanced as I am? I have sent my intended husband to look after my lover—the man of my father's choice is gone to bring me the man of my own: but how dispiriting is this interval of expectation!

SONG.

What bard, O Time, discover,
With wings first made thee move?
Ah! sure it was some lover
Who ne'er had left his love!
For who that once did prove
The pangs which absence brings,
Though but one day He were away,
Could picture thee with wings?
What bard, &c.

Enter DON CARLOS.

So, friend, is Antonio found?

Don Car. I could not meet with him, lady; but I doubt not my friend Isaac will be here with him presently.

Don. Louisa. Oh, shame! you have used no diligence. Is this your courtesy to a lady, who has trusted herself to your protection?

Don Car. Indeed, madam, I have not been remiss.

Don. Louisa. Well, well; but if either of you had known how each moment of delay weighs upon the heart of her who loves, and waits the object of her love, oh, ye would not then have trifled thus!

Don Car. Alas, I know it well!

Don. Louisa. Were you ever in love, then?

Don Car. I was, lady; but, while I have life, I will never be again.

Don. Louisa. Was your mistress so cruel?

Don Car. If she had always been so, I should have been happier.

SONG.

Oh, had my love ne'er smiled on me,
I ne'er had known such anguish;
But think how false, how cruel she,
To bid me cease to languish;
To bid me hope her hand to gain,
Breathe on a flame half perish'd;
And then with cold and fixed disdain,
To kill the hope she cherish'd.

Not worse his fate, who on a wreck,
That drove as winds did blow it,
Silent had left the shatter'd deck,
To find a grave below it.
Then land was cried—no more resign'd,
He glow'd with joy to hear it;
Not worse his fate, his woe, to find
The wreck must sink ere near it!

Don. Louisa. As I live, here is your friend coming with Antonio! I'll retire for a moment to surprise him. [*Exit.*]

Enter ISAAC *and* DON ANTONIO.

Don Ant. Indeed, my good friend, you must be mistaken. Clara d'Almanza in love with me, and employ you to bring me to meet her! It is impossible!

Isaac. That you shall see in an instant. Carlos, where is the lady?—[DON CARLOS *points to the door.*] In the next room, is she?

Don Ant. Nay, if that lady is really here, she certainly wants me to conduct her to a dear friend of mine, who has long been her lover.

Isaac. Psha! I tell you 'tis no such thing—you are the man she wants, and nobody but you. Here's ado to persuade you to take a pretty girl that's dying for you!

Don Ant. But I have no affection for this lady.

Isaac. And you have for Louisa, hey? But take my word for it, Antonio, you have no chance there—so you may as well secure the good that offers itself to you.

Don Ant. And could you reconcile it to your conscience to supplant your friend?

Isaac. Pish! Conscience has no more to do with gallantry than it has with politics. Why, you are no honest fellow if love can't make a rogue of you; so come—do go in and speak to her, at least.

Don Ant, Well, I have no objection to that.

Isaac. [*Opens the door.*] There—there she is—yonder by the window—get in, do.—[*Pushes him in, and half shuts the door.*] Now, Carlos, now I shall hamper him, I warrant! Stay, I'll peep how they go on. Egad, he looks confoundedly posed! Now she's coaxing him. See, Carlos, he begins to come to—ay, ay, he'll soon forget his conscience.

Don Car. Look—now they are both laughing!

Isaac. Ay, so they are—yes, yes, they are laughing at that dear friend he talked of—ay, poor devil, they have outwitted him.

Don Car, Now he's kissing her hand.

Isaac, Yes, yes, faith, they're agreed—he's caught, he's entangled. My dear Carlos, we have brought it about. Oh, this little cunning head! I'm a Machiavel—a very Machiavel!

Don Car, I hear somebody inquiring for you—I'll see who it is. [*Exit.*]

Re-enter DON ANTONIO *and* DONNA LOUISA.

Don Ant. Well, my good friend, this lady has so entirely convinced me of the certainty of your success at Don Jerome's, that I now resign my pretensions there.

Isaac. You never did a wiser thing, believe me; and, as for deceiving your friend, that's nothing at all—tricking is all fair in love, isn't it, ma'am?

Don. Louisa. Certainly, sir; and I am particularly glad to find you are of that opinion.

Isaac. O Lud! yes, ma'am—let any one outwit me that can, I say! But here, let me join your hands. There you lucky rogue! I wish you happily married from the bottom of my soul!

Don. Louisa. And I am sure, if you wish it, no one else should prevent it.

Isaac. Now, Antonio, we are rivals no more; so let us be friends, will you?

Don Ant. With all my heart, Isaac.

Isaac. It is not every man, let me tell you, that would have taken such pains, or been so generous to a rival.

Don Ant. No, 'faith, I don't believe there's another beside yourself in all Spain.

Isaac. Well, but you resign all pretensions to the other lady?

Don Ant. That I do, most sincerely.

Isaac. I doubt you have a little hankering there still.

Don Ant. None in the least, upon my soul.

Isaac. I mean after her fortune.

Don Ant. No, believe me. You are heartily welcome to every thing she has.

Isaac. Well, i'faith, you have the best of the bargain, as to beauty, twenty to one. Now I'll tell you a secret—I am to carry off Louisa this very evening.

Don. Louisa. Indeed!

Isaac. Yes, she has sworn not to take a husband from her father's hand—so I've persuaded him to trust her to walk with me in the garden, and then we shall give him the slip.

Don. Louisa. And is Don Jerome to know nothing of this?

Isaac. O Lud, no! there lies the jest. Don't you see that, by this step, I over-reach him? I shall be entitled to the girl's fortune, without settling a ducat on her. Ha! ha! ha! I'm a cunning dog, an't I? a sly little villain, eh?

Don Ant. Ha! ha! ha! you are indeed!

Isaac. Roguish, you'll say, but keen, eh? devilish keen?

Don Ant. So you are indeed—keen—very keen.

Isaac. And what a laugh we shall have at Don Jerome's when the truth comes out I hey?

Don. Louisa. Yes, I'll answer for it, we shall have a good laugh, when the truth comes out, Ha! ha! ha!

Re-enter DON CARLOS.

Don Car. Here are the dancers come to practise the fandango you intended to have honoured Donna Louisa with.

Isaac. Oh, I shan't want them; but, as I must pay them, I'll see a caper for my money. Will you excuse me?

Don. Louisa. Willingly.

Isaac. Here's my friend, whom you may command for any service. Madam, our most obedient—Antonio, I wish you all happiness.—[*Aside.*] Oh, the easy blockhead! what a tool I have made of him!—This was a masterpiece! [*Exit.*]

Don. Louisa. Carlos, will you be my guard again, and convey me to the convent of St. Catherine?

Don Ant. Why, Louisa—why should you go there?

Don. Louisa. I have my reasons, and you must not be seen to go with me; I shall write from thence to my father; perhaps, when he finds what he has driven me to, he may relent.

Don Ant. I have no hope from him. O Louisa! in these arms should be your sanctuary.

Don. Louisa. Be patient but for a little while—my father cannot force me from thence. But let me see you there before evening, and I will explain myself.

Don Ant. I shall obey.

Don. Louisa. Come, friend. Antonio, Carlos has been a lover himself.

Don Ant. Then he knows the value of his trust.

Don Car. You shall not find me unfaithful.

TRIO.

Soft pity never leaves the gentle breast
Where love has been received a welcome guest;
As wandering saints poor huts have sacred made,
He hallows every heart he once has sway'd,
And, when his presence we no longer share,
Still leaves compassion as a relic there. [*Exeunt.*]

ACT III.

SCENE I.—*A Library in* **DON JEROME'S** *House.*

Enter_ DON JEROME *and* SERVANT.

Don Jer. Why, I never was so amazed in my life! Louisa gone off with Isaac Mendoza! What! steal away with the very man whom I wanted her to marry—elope with her own husband, as it were—it is impossible!

Ser. Her maid says, sir, they had your leave to walk in the garden, while you were abroad. The door by the shrubbery was found open, and they have not been heard of since. [*Exit.*]

Don Jer. Well, it is the most unaccountable affair! 'sdeath! there is certainly some infernal mystery in it I can't comprehend!

Enter SECOND SERVANT, *with a letter.*

Ser. Here is a letter, sir, from Signor Isaac. [*Exit.*]

Don Jer. So, so, this will explain—ay, Isaac Mendoza—let me see— [*Reads.*]

_Dearest Sir,

You must, doubtless, be much surprised at my flight with your daughter!_—yes, 'faith, and well I may—*I had the happiness to gain her heart at our first interview*—The devil you had!—*But, she having unfortunately made a vow not to receive a husband from your hands, I was obliged to comply with her whim!*—So, so!—*We shall shortly throw ourselves at your feet, and I hope you will have a blessing ready for one, who will then be your son-in-law.* ISAAC MENDOZA.

A whim, hey? Why, the devil's in the girl, I think! This morning, she would die sooner than have him, and before evening she runs away with him! Well, well, my will's accomplished—let the motive be what it will—and the Portuguese, sure, will never deny to fulfil the rest of the article.

Re-enter SERVANT, *with another letter.*

Ser. Sir, here's a man below, who says he brought this from my young lady, Donna Louisa. [*Exit.*]

Don Jer. How! yes, it's my daughter's hand, indeed! Lord, there was no occasion for them both to write; well, let's see what she says— [*Reads.*]

_My dearest father,

How shall I entreat your pardon for the rash step I have taken—how confess the motive?_—Pish! hasn't Isaac just told me the motive?—onc would think they weren't together when they wrote.—*If I have a spirit too resentful of ill usage, I have also a heart as easily affected by kindness.*—So, so, here the whole matter comes out; her resentment for Antonio's ill usage has made her sensible of Isaac's kindness—yes, yes, it is all plain enough. Well. *I am not married yet, though with a man who, I am convinced, adores me.*—Yes, yes, I dare say Isaac is very fond of her. *But I shall anxiously expect your answer, in which, should I be so fortunate as to receive your consent, you will make completely happy your ever affectionate daughter,* LOUISA.

My consent! to be sure she shall have it! Egad, I was never better pleased—I have fulfilled my resolution—I knew I should. Oh, there's nothing like obstinacy! Lewis! [*Calls.*]

Re-enter SERVANT.

Let the man who brought the last letter, wait; and get me a pen and ink below.—[*Exit* SERVANT.] I am impatient to set poor Louisa's heart at rest. [*Calls.*]Holloa! Lewis! Sancho!

Enter SERVANTS.

See that there be a noble supper provided in the saloon to-night; serve up my best wines, and let me have music, d'ye hear?

Ser. Yes, sir.

Don Jer. And order all my doors to be thrown open; admit all guests, with masks or without masks.—[*Exeunt* SERVANTS.] I'faith, we'll have a night of it! and I'll let them see how merry an old man can be.

SONG.

Oh, the days when I was young.
When I laugh'd in fortune's spite;
Talk'd of love the whole day long,
And with nectar crown'd the night!
Then it was, old Father Care,
Little reck'd I of thy frown;
Half thy malice youth could bear,
And the rest a bumper drown.

Truth, they say, lies in a well,
Why, I vow I ne'er could see;
Let the water-drinkers tell,
There it always lay for me.
For when sparkling wine went round,
Never saw I falsehood's mask;
But still honest truth I found
In the bottom of each flask.

True, at length my vigour's flown,
I have years to bring decay;
Few the locks that now I own,
And the few I have are grey.
Yet, old Jerome, thou mayst boast,
While thy spirits do not tire;
Still beneath thy age's frost
Glows a spark of youthful fire. [*Exit*.]

SCENE II.—*The New Piazza.*

Enter DON FERDINAND *and* LOPEZ.

Don Ferd. What, could you gather no tidings of her? nor guess where she was gone? O Clara! Clara!

Lop. In truth, sir, I could not. That she was run away from her father, was in everybody's mouth; and that Don Guzman was in pursuit of her, was also a very common report. Where she was gone, or what was become of her, no one could take upon them to say.

Don Ferd. 'Sdeath and fury, you blockhead! she can't be out of Seville.

Lop. So I said to myself, sir. 'Sdeath and fury, you blockhead, says I, she can't be out of Seville. Then some said, she had hanged herself for love; and others have it, Don Antonio had carried her off.

Don Ferd. 'Tis false, scoundrel! no one said that.

Lop. Then I misunderstood them, sir.

Don Ferd. Go, fool, get home! and never let me see you again till you bring me news of her.—[*Exit* LOPEZ.] Oh, how my fondness for this ungrateful girl has hurt my disposition.

Enter ISAAC.

Isaac. So, I have her safe, and have only to find a priest to marry us. Antonio now may marry Clara, or not, if he pleases.

Don Ferd. What! what was that you said of Clara?

Isaac. Oh, Ferdinand! my brother-in-law that shall be, who thought of meeting you?

Don Ferd. But what of Clara?

Isaac. I'faith, you shall hear. This morning, as I was coming down, I met a pretty damsel, who told me her name was Clara d'Almanza, and begged my protection.

Don Ferd. How!

Isaac. She said she had eloped from her father, Don Guzman, but that love for a young gentleman in Seville was the cause.

Don Ferd. Oh, Heavens! did she confess it?

Isaac. Oh, yes, she confessed at once. But then, says she, my lover is not informed of my flight, nor suspects my intention.

Don Ferd. [*Aside*.] Dear creature! no more I did indeed! Oh, I am the happiest fellow! – [*Aloud*.] Well, Isaac?

Isaac. Why then she entreated me to find him out for her, and bring him to her.

Don Ferd. Good Heavens, how lucky! Well, come along, let's lose no time. [*Pulling him*.]

Isaac. Zooks! where are we to go?

Don Ferd. Why, did anything more pass?

Isaac. Anything more! yes; the end on't was, that I was moved with her speeches, and complied with her desires.

Don Ferd. Well and where is she?

Isaac. Where is she? why, don't I tell you? I complied with her request, and left her safe in the arms of her lover.

Don Ferd. 'Sdeath, you trifle with me! – I have never seen her.

Isaac. You! O Lud no! how the devil should you? 'Twas Antonio she wanted; and with Antonio I left her.

Don Ferd. [*Aside*.] Hell and madness! – [*Aloud*.] What, Antonio d'Ercilla?

Isaac. Ay, ay, the very man; and the best part of it was, he was shy of taking her at first. He talked a good deal about honour, and conscience, and deceiving some dear friend; but, Lord, we soon overruled that!

Don Ferd. You did!

Isaac. Oh, yes, presently.—Such deceit! says he.—Pish! says the lady, tricking is all fair in love. But then, my friend, says he.— Psha! damn your friend, says I. So, poor wretch, he has no chance.— No, no; he may hang himself as soon as he pleases.

Don Ferd. [*Aside.*] I must go, or I shall betray myself.

Isaac. But stay, Ferdinand, you han't heard the best of the joke.

Don Ferd. Curse on your joke!

Isaac. Good lack! what's the matter now? I thought to have diverted you.

Don Ferd. Be racked! tortured! damned!

Isaac. Why, sure you are not the poor devil of a lover, are you?—I'faith, as sure as can be, he is! This is a better joke than t'other. Ha! ha! ha!

Don Ferd. What! do you laugh? you vile, mischievous varlet!—[*Collars him.*] But that you're beneath my anger, I'd tear your heart out! [*Throws him from him.*]

Isaac. O mercy! here's usage for a brother-in-law!

Don Ferd. But, hark ye, rascal! tell me directly where these false friends are gone, or, by my soul— —[*Draws.*]

Isaac. For Heaven's sake, now, my dear brother-in-law, don't be in a rage! I'll recollect as well as I can.

Don Ferd. Be quick, then!

Isaac. I will, I will!—but people's memories differ; some have a treacherous memory: now mine is a cowardly memory—it takes to its heels at sight of a drawn sword—it does i'faith; and I could as soon fight as recollect.

Don Ferd. Zounds! tell me the truth, and I won't hurt you.

Isaac. No, no, I know you won't, my dear brother-in-law; but that ill-looking thing there— —

Don Ferd. What, then, you won't tell me?

Isaac. Yes, yes, I will; I'll tell you all, upon my soul!—but why need you listen, sword in hand?

Don Ferd. Why, there.—[*Puts up.*] Now.

Isaac. Why, then, I believe they are gone to—that is, my friend Carlos told me he had left Donna Clara—dear Ferdinand, keep your hands off—at the convent of St. Catherine.

Don Ferd. St. Catherine!

Isaac. Yes; and that Antonio was to come to her there.

Don Ferd. Is this the truth?

Isaac. It is indeed; and all I know, as I hope for life!

Don Ferd. Well, coward, take your life; 'tis that false, dishonourable Antonio, who shall feel my vengeance.

Isaac. Ay, ay, kill him; cut his throat, and welcome.

Don Ferd. But, for Clara! infamy on her! she is not worth my resentment.

Isaac. No more she is, my dear brother-in-law. I'faith I would not be angry about her; she is not worth it, indeed.

Don Ferd. 'Tis false! she is worth the enmity of princes!

Isaac. True, true, so she is; and I pity you exceedingly for having lost her.

Don Ferd. 'Sdeath, you rascal! how durst you talk of pitying me?

Isaac. Oh, dear brother-in-law, I beg pardon! I don't pity you in the least, upon my soul!

Don Ferd. Get hence, fool, and provoke me no further; nothing but your insignificance saves you!

Isaac. [*Aside.*] I'faith, then, my insignificance is the best friend I have.—[*Aloud.*] I'm going, dear Ferdinand.—[*Aside.*] What a curst hot hot-headed bully it is! [*Exeunt severally.*]

SCENE III.—*The Garden of the Convent.*

Enter DONNA LOUISA *and* DONNA CLARA.

Don. Louisa. And you really wish my brother may not find you out?

Don. Clara. Why else have I concealed myself under this disguise?

Don. Louisa. Why, perhaps because the dress becomes you: for you certainly don't intend to be a nun for life.

Don. Clara. If, indeed, Ferdinand had not offended me so last night—

Don. Louisa. Come, come, it was his fear of losing you made him so rash.

Don. Clara. Well, you may think me cruel, but I swear, if he were here this instant, I believe I should forgive him.

SONG.

By him we love offended,
How soon our anger flies!
One day apart, 'tis ended;
Behold him, and it dies.

Last night, your roving brother,
Enraged, I bade depart;
And sure his rude presumption
Deserved to lose my heart.

Yet, were he now before met
In spite of injured pride,
I fear my eyes would pardon

Before my tongue could chide.

Don. Louisa. I protest, Clara, I shall begin to think you are seriously resolved to enter on your probation.

Don. Clara. And, seriously, I very much doubt whether the character of a nun would not become me best.

Don. Louisa. Why, to be sure, the character of a nun is a very becoming one at a masquerade: but no pretty woman, in her senses, ever thought of taking the veil for above a night.

Don. Clara. Yonder I see your Antonio is returned—I shall only interrupt you; ah, Louisa, with what happy eagerness you turn to look for him! [*Exit.*]

Enter DON ANTONIO.

Don Ant. Well, my Louisa, any news since I left you?

Don. Louisa. None. The messenger is not yet returned from my father.

Don Ant. Well, I confess, I do not perceive what we are to expect from him.

Don. Louisa. I shall be easier, however, in having made the trial: I do not doubt your sincerity, Antonio; but there is a chilling air around poverty, that often kills affection, that was not nursed in it. If we would make love our household god, we had best secure him a comfortable roof.

SONG.—*Don Antonio.*

How oft, Louisa, hast thou told,
(Nor wilt thou the fond boast disown,)
Thou wouldst not lose Antonio's love
To reign the partner of a throne!
And by those lips that spoke so kind,
And by that hand I've press'd to mine,
To be the lord of wealth and power,

By heavens, I would not part with thine!

Then how, my soul, can we be poor,
Who own what kingdoms could not buy?
Of this true heart thou shalt be queen,
In serving thee, a monarch I.
Thus uncontroll'd, in mutual bliss,
I rich in love's exhaustless mine,
Do thou snatch treasures from my lips,
And I'll take kingdoms back from thine!

Enter MAID *with a letter.*

Don. Louisa. My father's answer, I suppose.

Don Ant. My dearest Louisa, you may be assured that it contains nothing but threats and reproaches.

Don. Louisa. Let us see, however.—[Reads.] *Dearest daughter, make your lover happy: you have my full consent to marry as your whim has chosen, but be sure come home and sup with your affectionate father.*

Don Ant. You jest, Louisa!

Don. Louisa. [*Gives him the letter.*.] Read! read!

Don Ant. 'Tis so, by heavens! Sure there must be some mistake; but that's none of our business.—Now, Louisa, you have no excuse for delay.

Don. Louisa. Shall we not then return and thank my father?

Don Ant. But first let the priest put it out of his power to recall his word.—I'll fly to procure one.

Don. Louisa. Nay, if you part with me again, perhaps you may lose me.

Don Ant. Come, then—there is a friar of a neighbouring convent is my friend; you have already been diverted by the manners of a nunnery; let us see whether there is less hypocrisy among the holy fathers.

Don. Louisa. I'm afraid not, Antonio—for in religion, as in friendship, they who profess most are the least sincere. [*Exeunt.*]

Re-enter DONNA CLARA.

Don. Clara, So, yonder they go, as happy as a mutual and confessed affection can make them, while I am left in solitude. Heigho! love may perhaps excuse the rashness of an elopement from one's friend, but I am sure nothing but the presence of the man we love can support it. Ha! what do I see! Ferdinand, as I live! How could he gain admission? By potent gold, I suppose, as Antonio did. How eager and disturbed he seems! He shall not know me as yet. [*Lets down her veil.*]

Enter DON FERDINAND.

Don Ferd. Yes, those were certainly they—my information was right. [*Going.*]

Don. Clara. [*Stops him.*] Pray, signor, what is your business here?

Don Ferd. No matter—no matter! Oh! they stop.—[*Looks out.*] Yes, that is the perfidious Clara indeed!

Don. Clara. So, a jealous error—I'm glad to see him so moved. [*Aside.*]

Don Ferd. Her disguise can't conceal her—no, no, I know her too well.

Don. Clara. [*Aside.*] Wonderful discernment!—[*Aloud.*] But, signor——

Don Ferd. Be quiet, good nun; don't tease me!—By heavens, she leans upon his arm, hangs fondly on it! O woman, woman!

Don. Clar. But, signor, who is it you want?

Don Ferd. Not you, not you, so prythee don't tease me. Yet pray stay—gentle nun, was it not Donna Clara d'Almanza just parted from you?

Don. Clara. Clara d'Almanza, signor, is not yet out of the garden.

Don Ferd. Ay, ay, I knew I was right! And pray is not that gentleman, now at the porch with her, Antonio d'Ercilla?

Don. Clara. It is indeed, signor.

Don Ferd. So, so; but now one question more—can you inform me for what purpose they have gone away?

Don. Clara. They are gone to be married, I believe.

Don Ferd. Very well—enough. Now if I don't mar their wedding! [*Exit.*]

Don. Clara. [*Unveils.*] I thought jealousy had made lovers quick-sighted, but it has made mine blind. Louisa's story accounts to me for this error, and I am glad to find I have power enough over him to make him so unhappy. But why should not I be present at his surprise when undeceived? When he's through the porch, I'll follow him; and, perhaps, Louisa shall not singly be a bride.

SONG.

Adieu, thou dreary pile, where never dies
The sullen echo of repentant sighs!
Ye sister mourners of each lonely cell
Inured to hymns and sorrow, fare ye well!
For happier scenes I fly this darksome grove,
To saints a prison, but a tomb to love! [*Exit.*]

SCENE IV.—*A Court before the Priory.*

Enter ISAAC, *crossing the stage*, DON ANTONIO *following*.

Don Ant. What, my friend Isaac!

Isaac. What, Antonio! wish me joy! I have Louisa safe.

Don Ant. Have you? I wish you joy with all my soul.

Isaac. Yes, I come here to procure a priest to marry us.

Don Ant. So, then, we are both on the same errand; I am come to look for Father Paul.

Isaac. Ha! I'm glad on't—but, i'faith, he must tack me first; my love is waiting.

Don Ant. So is mine—I left her in the porch.

Isaac. Ay, but I'm in haste to go back to Don Jerome.

Don Ant. And so am I too.

Isaac. Well, perhaps he'll save time, and marry us both together—or I'll be your father, and you shall be mine. Come along—but you are obliged to me for all this.

Don Ant. Yes, yes. [*Exeunt*.]

SCENE V.—*A Room in the Priory.*

FATHER PAUL, FATHER FRANCIS, FATHER AUGUSTINE, *and other* FRIARS, *discovered at a table drinking.*

GLEE AND CHORUS.

This bottle's the sun of our table,
His beams are rosy wine
We, planets, that are not able
Without his help to shine.
Let mirth and glee abound!
You'll soon grow bright
With borrow'd light,
And shine as he goes round.

Paul. Brother Francis, toss the bottle about, and give me your toast.

Fran. Have we drunk the Abbess of St. Ursuline?

Paul. Yes, yes; she was the last.

Fran. Then I'll give you the blue-eyed nun of St. Catherine's.

Paul. With all my heart.—[*Drinks.*] Pray, brother Augustine, were there any benefactions left in my absence?

Aug. Don Juan Corduba has left a hundred ducats, to remember him in our masses.

Paul. Has he? let them be paid to our wine-merchant, and we'll remember him in our cups, which will do just as well. Anything more?

Aug. Yes; Baptista, the rich miser, who died last week, has bequeathed us a thousand pistoles, and the silver lamp he used in his own chamber, to burn before the image of St. Anthony.

Paul. 'Twas well meant, but we'll employ his money better— Baptista's bounty shall light the living, not the dead. St. Anthony is not afraid to be left in the dark, though he was.—[*Knocking.*] See who's there.

[FATHER FRANCIS *goes to the door and opens it.*]

Enter PORTER.

Port. Here's one without, in pressing haste to speak with Father Paul.

Fran. Brother Paul!

[FATHER PAUL *comes from behind a curtain with a glass of wine, and in his hand a piece of cake.*]

Paul. Here! how durst you, fellow, thus abruptly break in upon our devotions?

Port. I thought they were finished.

Paul. No, they were not—were they, brother Francis?

Fran. Not by a bottle each.

Paul. But neither you nor your fellows mark how the hours go; no, you mind nothing but the gratifying of your appetites; ye eat, and swill, and sleep, and gourmandise, and thrive, while we are wasting in mortification.

Port. We ask no more than nature craves.

Paul. 'Tis false, ye have more appetites than hairs! and your flushed, sleek, and pampered appearance is the disgrace of our order— out on't! If you are hungry, can't you be content with the wholesome roots of the earth? and if you are dry, isn't there the crystal spring?—[*Drinks.*] Put this away,—[*Gives the glass*] and show me where I am wanted.—[PORTER *drains the glass.*—PAUL, *going, turns.*] So you would have drunk it if there had been any left! Ah, glutton! glutton! [*Exeunt.*]

SCENE VI.—*The Court before the Priory.*

Enter ISAAC *and* DON ANTONIO.

Isaac. A plaguey while coming, this same father Paul.—He's detained at vespers, I suppose, poor fellow.

Don Ant. No, here he comes.

Enter FATHER PAUL.

Good father Paul, I crave your blessing.

Isaac. Yes, good father Paul, we are come to beg a favour.

Paul. What is it, pray?

Isaac. To marry us, good father Paul; and in truth thou dost look like the priest of Hymen.

Paul. In short, I may be called so; for I deal in repentance and mortification.

Isaac. No, no, thou seemest an officer of Hymen, because thy presence speaks content and good humour.

Paul. Alas, my appearance is deceitful. Bloated I am, indeed! for fasting is a windy recreation, and it hath swollen me like a bladder.

Don Ant. But thou hast a good fresh colour in thy face, father; rosy, i'faith!

Paul. Yes, I have blushed for mankind, till the hue of my shame is as fixed as their vices.

Isaac. Good man!

Paul. And I have laboured, too, but to what purpose? they continue to sin under my very nose.

Isaac. Efecks, father, I should have guessed as much, for your nose seems to be put to the blush more than any other part of your face.

Paul. Go, you're a wag.

Don Ant. But to the purpose, father—will you officiate for us?

Paul. To join young people thus clandestinely is not safe: and, indeed, I have in my heart many weighty reasons against it.

Don Ant. And I have in my hand many weighty reasons for it. Isaac, haven't you an argument or two in our favour about you?

Isaac. Yes, yes; here is a most unanswerable purse.

Paul. For shame! you make me angry: you forget who I am, and when importunate people have forced their trash—ay, into this pocket here— or into this—why, then the sin was theirs.—[*They put money into his pockets*.] Fie, now how you distress me! I would return it, but that I must touch it that way, and so wrong my oath.

Don Ant. Now then, come with us.

Isaac. Ay, now give us our title to joy and rapture.

Paul. Well, when your hour of repentance comes, don't blame me.

Don Ant. [*Aside*.] No bad caution to my friend Isaac.—[*Aloud*.] Well, well, father, do you do your part, and I'll abide the consequences.

Isaac. Ay, and so will I.

Enter DONNA LOUISA, *running*.

Don. Louisa. O Antonio, Ferdinand is at the porch, and inquiring for us.

Isaac. Who? Don Ferdinand! he's not inquiring for me, I hope.

Don Ant. Fear not, my love; I'll soon pacify him.

Isaac. Egad, you won't. Antonio, take my advice, and run away; this Ferdinand is the most unmerciful dog, and has the cursedest long sword! and, upon my, soul, he comes on purpose to cut your throat.

Don Ant. Never fear, never fear.

Isaac. Well, you may stay if you will; but I'll get some one to marry me: for by St. Iago, he shall never meet me again, while I am master of a pair of heels. [*Runs out.*—DONNA LOUISA *lets down her veil.*]

Enter DON FERDINAND.

Don Ferd. So, sir, I have met with you at last.

Don Ant. Well, sir.

Don Ferd. Base, treacherous man! whence can a false, deceitful soul, like yours, borrow confidence, to look so steadily on the man you've injured!

Don Ant. Ferdinand, you are too warm: 'tis true you find me on the point of wedding one I loved beyond my life; but no argument of mine prevailed on her to elope.—I scorn deceit, as much as you. By heaven I knew not that she had left her father's till I saw her!

Don Ferd. What a mean excuse! You have wronged your friend, then, for one, whose wanton forwardness anticipated your treachery—of this, indeed, your Jew pander informed me; but let your conduct be consistent, and since you have dared to do a wrong, follow me, and show you have a spirit to avow it.

Don. Louisa. Antonio, I perceive his mistake—leave him to me.

Paul. Friend, you are rude, to interrupt the union of two willing hearts.

Don Ferd. No, meddling priest! the hand he seeks is mine.

Paul. If so, I'll proceed no further. Lady, did you ever promise this youth your hand? [*To* DONNA LOUISA, *who shakes her head.*]

Don Ferd. Clara, I thank you for your silence—I would not have heard your tongue avow such falsity; be't your punishment to remember that I have not reproached you.

Enter DONNA CLARA, *veiled.*

Don. Clara. What mockery is this?

Don Ferd. Antonio, you are protected now, but we shall meet. [*Going,* DONNA CLARA *holds one arm, and* DONNA LOUISA *the other.*]

DUET.

Don. Louisa.
Turn thee round, I pray thee,
Calm awhile thy rage.

Don. Clara.
I must help to stay thee,
And thy wrath assuage.

Don. Louisa.
Couldst thou not discover
One so dear to thee?

Don. Clara.
Canst thou be a lover,
And thus fly from me? [*Both unveil.*]

Don Ferd. How's this? My sister! Clara, too—I'm confounded.

Don. Louisa. 'Tis even so, good brother.

Paul. How! what impiety? did the man want to marry his own sister?

Don. Louisa. And ar'n't you ashamed of yourself not to know your own sister?

Don. Clara. To drive away your own mistress— —

Don. Louisa. Don't you see how jealousy blinds people?

Don. Clara. Ay, and will you ever be jealous again?

Don Ferd. Never—never!—You, sister, I know will forgive me—but how, Clara, shall I presume— —

Don. Clara. No, no; just now you told me not to tease you—"Who do you want, good signor?" "Not you, not you!" Oh you blind wretch! but swear never to be jealous again, and I'll forgive you.

Don Ferd. By all— —

Don. Clara. There, that will do—you'll keep the oath just as well. [*Gives her hand.*]

Don. Louisa. But, brother, here is one to whom some apology is due.

Don Ferd. Antonio, I am ashamed to think— —

Don Ant. Not a word of excuse, Ferdinand—I have not been in love myself without learning that a lover's anger should never be resented. But come—let us retire, with this good father, and we'll explain to you the cause of this error.

GLEE AND CHORUS.

Oft does Hymen smile to hear
Wordy vows of feign'd regard;
Well, he knows when they're sincere,
Never slow to give reward
For his glory is to prove
Kind to those who wed for love. [*Exeunt.*]

SCENE VII—*A Grand Saloon in* DON JEROME'S *House.*

Enter DON JEROME, LOPEZ, *and* SERVANTS.

Don Jer. Be sure, now, let everything be in the best order—let all my servants have on their merriest faces: but tell them to get as little drunk as possible, till after supper.—[*Exeunt* SERVANTS.] So, Lopez, where's your master? shan't we have him at supper?

Lop. Indeed, I believe not, sir—he's mad, I doubt! I'm sure he has frighted me from him.

Don Jer. Ay, ay, he's after some wench, I suppose: a young rake! Well, well, we'll be merry without him. [*Exit* LOPEZ.]

Enter a SERVANT.

Ser. Sir, here is Signor Isaac. [*Exit.*]

Enter ISAAC.

Don Jer. So, my dear son-in-law—there, take my blessing and forgiveness. But where's my daughter? where's Louisa?

Isaac. She's without, impatient for a blessing, but almost afraid to enter.

Don Jer. Oh, fly and bring her in.—[*Exit* ISAAC.] Poor girl, I long to see her pretty face.

Isaac. [*Without.*] Come, my, charmer! my trembling angel!

Re-enter ISAAC *with* DUENNA; DON JEROME *runs to meet them; she kneels.*

Don Jer. Come to my arms, my—[*Starts back.*] Why, who the devil have we here?

Isaac. Nay, Don Jerome, you promised her forgiveness; see how the dear creature droops!

Don Jer. Droops indeed! Why, Gad take me, this is old Margaret! But where's my daughter? where's Louisa?

Isaac. Why, here, before your eyes—nay, don't be abashed, my sweet wife!

Don Jer. Wife with a vengeance! Why, zounds! you have not married the Duenna!

Duen. [*Kneeling.*] Oh, dear papa! you'll not disown me, sure!

Don Jer. Papa! papa! Why, zounds! your impudence is as great as your ugliness!

Isaac. Rise, my charmer, go throw your snowy arms about his neck, and convince him you are— —

Duen. Oh, sir, forgive me! [*Embraces him.*]

Don Jer. Help! murder!

Enter SERVANTS.

Ser. What's the matter, sir?

Don Jer. Why, here, this damned Jew has brought an old harridan to strangle me.

Isaac. Lord, it is his own daughter, and he is so hard-hearted he won't forgive her!

Enter DON ANTONIO *and* DONNA LOUISA; *they kneel.*

Don Jer. Zounds and fury! what's here now? who sent for you, sir, and who the devil are you?

Don Ant. This lady's husband, sir.

Isaac. Ay, that he is, I'll be sworn; for I left them with a priest, and was to have given her away.

Don Jer. You were?

Isaac. Ay; that's my honest friend, Antonio; and that's the little girl I told you I had hampered him with.

Don Jer. Why, you are either drunk or mad—this is my daughter.

Isaac. No, no; 'tis you are both drunk and mad, I think—here's your daughter.

Don Jer. Hark ye, old iniquity! will you explain all this, or not?

Duen. Come then, Don Jerome, I will—though our habits might inform you all. Look on your daughter, there, and on me.

Isaac. What's this I hear?

Duen. The truth is, that in your passion this morning you made a small mistake; for you turned your daughter out of doors, and locked up your humble servant.

Isaac. O Lud! O Lud! here's a pretty fellow, to turn his daughter out of doors, instead of an old Duenna!

Don Jer. And, O Lud! O Lud! here's a pretty fellow, to marry an old Duenna instead of my daughter! But how came the rest about?

Duen. I have only to add, that I remained in your daughter's place, and had the good fortune to engage the affections of my sweet husband here.

Isaac. Her husband! why, you old witch, do you think I'll be your husband now? This is a trick, a cheat! and you ought all to be ashamed of yourselves.

Don Ant. Hark ye, Isaac, do you dare to complain of tricking? Don Jerome, I give you my word, this cunning Portuguese has brought all this upon himself, by endeavouring to overreach you, by getting your daughter's fortune, without making any settlement in return.

Don Jer. Overreach me!

Don. Louisa. 'Tis so, indeed, sir, and we can prove it to you.

Don Jer. Why, Gad, take me, it must be so, or he never could put up with such a face as Margaret's—so, little Solomon, I wish you joy of your wife, with all my soul.

Don. Louisa. Isaac, tricking is all fair in love—let you alone for the plot!

Don Ant. A cunning dog, ar'n't you? A sly little villain, eh?

Don. Louisa. Roguish, perhaps; but keen, devilish keen!

Don Jer. Yes, yes; his aunt always called him little Solomon.

Isaac. Why, the plagues of Egypt upon you all! but do you think I'll submit to such an imposition?

Don Ant. Isaac, one serious word—you'd better be content as you are; for, believe me, you will find that, in the opinion of the world, there is not a fairer subject for contempt and ridicule than a knave become the dupe of his own art.

Isaac. I don't care—I'll not endure this. Don Jerome, 'tis you have done this—you would be so cursed positive about the beauty of her you locked up, and all the time I told you she was as old as my mother, and as ugly as the devil.

Duen. Why, you little insignificant reptile!— —

Don Jer. That's right!—attack him, Margaret.

Duen. Dare such a thing as you pretend to talk of beauty?—A walking rouleau?—a body that seems to owe all its consequence to the dropsy! a pair of eyes like two dead beetles in a wad of brown dough! a beard like an artichoke, with dry, shrivelled jaws that would disgrace the mummy of a monkey?

Don Jer. Well done, Margaret!

Duen. But you shall know that I have a brother who wears a sword— and, if you don't do me justice—

Isaac. Fire seize your brother, and you too! I'll fly to Jerusalem to avoid you!

Duen. Fly where you will, I'll follow you.

Don Jer. Throw your snowy arms about him, Margaret.—[*Exeunt* ISAAC *and* DUENNA.] But, Louisa, are you really married to this modest gentleman?

Don. Louisa. Sir, in obedience to your commands, I gave him my hand within this hour.

Don Jer. My commands!

Don Ant. Yes, sir; here is your consent, under your own hand.

Don Jer. How! would you rob me of my child by a trick, a false pretence? and do you think to get her fortune by the same means? Why, 'slife! you are as great a rogue as Isaac!

Don Ant. No, Don Jerome; though I have profited by this paper in gaining your daughter's hand, I scorn to obtain her fortune by deceit. There, sir—[*Gives a letter.*] Now give her your blessing for a dower, and all the little I possess shall be settled on her in return. Had you wedded her to a prince, he could do no more.

Don Jer. Why, Gad, take me, but you are a very extraordinary fellow! But have you the impudence to suppose no one can do a generous action but yourself? Here, Louisa, tell this proud fool of yours that he's the only man I know that would renounce your fortune; and, by my soul! he's the only man in Spain that's worthy of it. There, bless you both: I'm an obstinate old fellow when I'm in the wrong; but you shall now find me as steady in the right.

Enter DON FERDINAND *and* DONNA CLARA.

Another wonder still! Why, sirrah! Ferdinand, you have not stole a nun, have you?

Don Fred. She is a nun in nothing but her habit, sir—look nearer, and you will perceive 'tis Clara d'Almanza, Don Guzman's daughter; and, with pardon for stealing a wedding, she is also my wife.

Don Jer. Gadsbud, and a great fortune! Ferdinand, you are a prudent young rogue, and I forgive you: and, ifecks, you are a pretty little damsel. Give your father-in-law a kiss, you smiling rogue!

Don. Clara. There, old gentleman; and now mind you behave well to us.

Don Jer. Ifecks, those lips ha'n't been chilled by kissing beads! Egad, I believe I shall grow the best-humoured fellow in Spain. Lewis! Sancho! Carlos! d'ye hear? are all my doors thrown open? Our children's weddings are the only holidays our age can boast; and then we drain, with pleasure, the little stock of spirits time has left us.—[*Music within.*] But, see, here come our friends and neighbours!

Enter MASQUERADERS.

And, i'faith, we'll make a night on't, with wine, and dance, and catches—then old and young shall join us.

FINALE.

Don Jer.
Come now for jest and smiling,
Both old and young beguiling,
Let us laugh and play, so blithe and gay,
Till we banish care away.

Don. Louisa.
Thus crown'd with dance and song,
The hours shall glide along,
With a heart at ease, merry, merry glees
Can never fail to please.

Don Ferd.
Each bride with blushes glowing,
Our wine as rosy flowing,
Let us laugh and play, so blithe and gay,
Till we banish care away.

Don Ant.
Then healths to every friend
The night's repast shall end,
With a heart at ease, merry, merry glees
Can never fail to please.

Don. Clar.
Nor, while we are so joyous,
Shall anxious fear annoy us;

Let us laugh and play, so blithe and gay,
Till we banish care away.

Don Jer.
For generous guests like these
Accept the wish to please,
So we'll laugh and play, so blithe and gay,
Your smiles drive care away.

[*Exeunt omnes.*]